Cat's Diary

Written by Jill Eggleton
Illustrated by Kelvin Hawley

ABOUT ME

Name Cat

Address 42 Ratroy Place

Phone 555-5621

Fax 555-5622

E-mail cat@ co.au

Vet Mr. Biggles

Vaccinations
Cat Flu, Cat Pox

Owner Max

Favorite Food Fish pie

Best Friend Moggy Jones

IMPORTANT EVENTS

My Birthday March 2

All Cats' Day February 14

Halloween October 31

Cat Show Day November 26

Max's Birthday April 9

Granny's Birthday July 6

That Dog's Birthday May 2

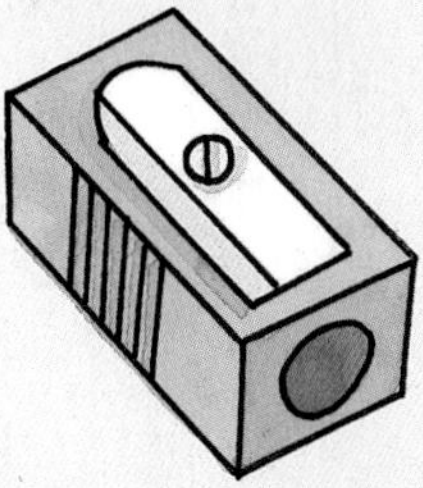

Sunday

Today, everybody went out. They took that dog with them, thank goodness. I could sleep in my chair all day. I didn't have that dog's wet nose waking me up. I was getting hungry by the time they came home. I'd tried to catch the fish, but it got away. I don't know why they keep that fish. It just swims around in the bowl. It never even stops to sleep! I'm glad I'm not a fish. It must be boring.

dumb fish

4

5

Monday

I had a TERRIBLE  day today. That dog is so mean. I was sleeping in my chair and he shook water all over my fur. I showed him my claws and he ran off. I think he is really scared of my claws. Good! Max made such a fuss over him. Max dried him with Granny's towel. I heard Granny saying she had dog hair all over her. I bet she wasn't happy that Max had used her towel.

hairy granny

Tuesday

I felt a bit sorry for that dog today. He was sneezing, so I thought I would be nice. I let him have my chair. He loved it, but he didn't say thank you. When you are sick you should still have manners! Cats can purr to say thank you, but dogs don't know how to purr.

9

Wednesday

angry granny

I should not have given that dog the chair yesterday. He was really mean to me again and chased me all over the yard. Poor Granny's yard is such a mess! She was mad at that dog. I had a good time chasing the birds. They flew off, making a lot of noise. You would think I had taken a feather! I might just try and get one next time. It would be a wonderful present for Granny.

stupid bird →

ROCHESTER ELEMENTARY SCHOOL

11

Thursday

weed →

Max's granny and that dog went out today. I tried to get the fish again, but I got my paws all tangled up in the silly weeds. It took me a long time to get them off. They made green marks on the rugs. Max's granny was really **angry** when she saw the mess. She asked me what I had been doing, but I didn't look at her. She didn't ask the fish. It is no use asking a fish. I will try hard to get her a feather tomorrow — or maybe she would like the whole bird!

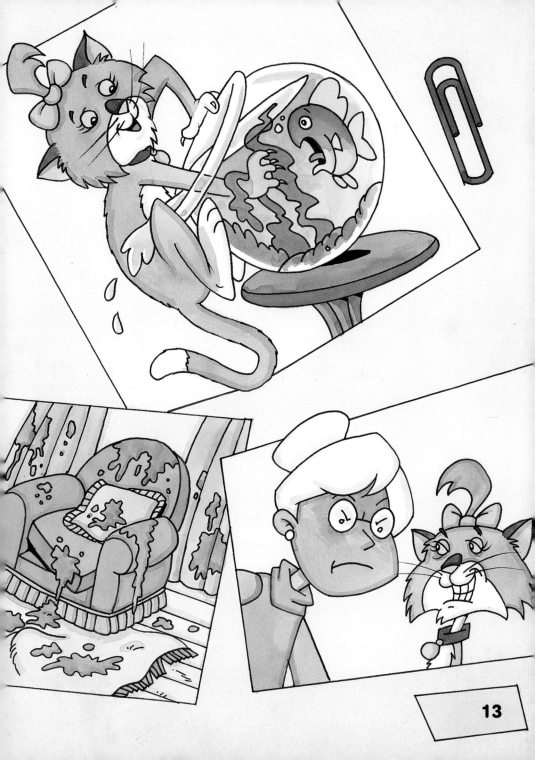

13

Friday

I had a really good day today. A nice dog came to visit. It was white with curly hair and it was friendly to me. It is good that not all dogs are mean. Max's granny was very upset about her garden. I think that dog dug up a rose bush so he could bury his bones. How selfish! I felt sorry for Max's granny. I tried to get her a feather, but those birds were too quick. But I went and slept on her bed. I hoped she liked that. I don't know if she did, because she said cats and dogs were just pests.

← nice dog

bone →

Saturday

I was home by myself again today. Max took that dog to the river. Sometimes I feel sorry for him. He has to do what Max says, but I can just please myself. I stayed in my chair for most of the day. I didn't try and get the fish again. There are new green weeds in the bowl now. Lots of them. I was hungry, so I opened the fridge and helped myself to some hot dogs. When that dog came home, he licked Max's granny. Yuck! I think he was trying to be clever. He had better not lick me! It would be terrible if I had to scratch his tongue!

Hot dogs, yum yum!

DIARIES

Diaries keep:

- a record of events
- a record of thoughts and feelings

My diary has events in sequence . . .

**Sunday Monday Tuesday
Wednesday Thursday
Friday Saturday**

18

My diary has private and personal thoughts.

I don't know why they keep that fish.

Even when you are sick, you should remember your manners.

I have decided that not all dogs are mean or ugly.

Sometimes I feel sorry for that dog.

19

Guide Notes

> **Title: Cat's Diary**
> **Stage:** Fluency (1)
>
> **Text Form:** Diary
> **Approach:** Guided Reading
> **Processes:** Thinking Critically, Exploring Language, Processing Information
> **Written and Visual Focus**: Diary, Thumbnail Sketches

THINKING CRITICALLY
(sample questions)
- How do you know what the cat feels about the dog?
- How do you know the cat likes Granny?
- How do you know the cat wasn't mean all the time?
- Why do you think the cat didn't try and get the fish on Saturday?
- Do you think the cat would want the dog to read its diary? Why/Why not?

EXPLORING LANGUAGE

Terminology
Spread, author and illustrator credits, ISBN number

Vocabulary
Clarify: vaccination, tangled, selfish
Nouns: birds, fish, bowl, cat, dog
Verbs: swim, jump, scratch, lick, chase, catch
Singular/plural: bird/birds, dog/dogs, bone/bones
Abbreviations: fax (facsimile), E-mail (electronic mail)

Print Conventions
Apostrophes – possessives (dog's nose, cat's tail), contraction (I'd)

Phonological Patterns
Focus on short and long vowel **o** (g**o**t, st**o**p, d**o**g, th**o**se, **o**ver)
Discuss root words – boring, dried, chasing
Look at suffix **ful** (wonder**ful**)